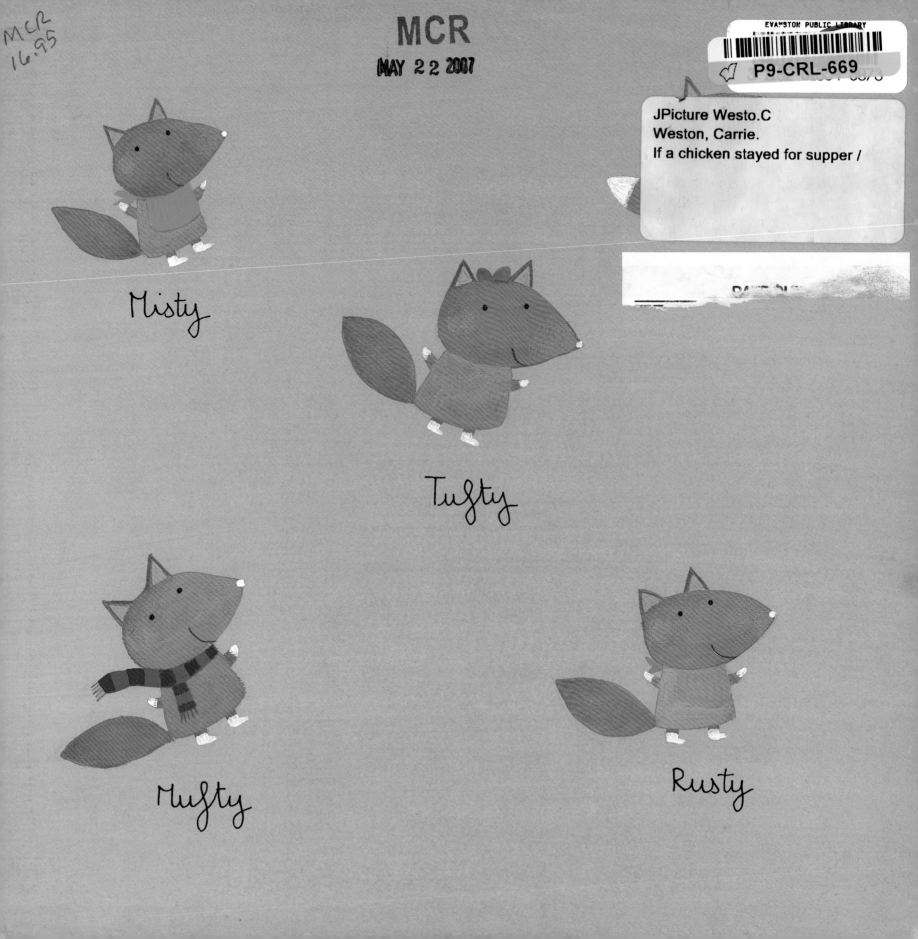

Misty

Tufty

Rufty

Rusty

For my Aunt Joan, who gave me poetry books
C. W.

For "Meraviglio" with tenderness
S. F.

Text copyright © 2006 Carrie Weston
Illustrations copyright © 2006 Sophie Fatus
First published in Great Britain in 2006 by Simon and Schuster UK Ltd
Africa House, 64-78 Kingsway, London WC2B 6AH, under the title *Chicken for Supper*
First published in the United States of America by Holiday House, Inc. in 2007
All Rights Reserved
Printed and Bound in China
www.holidayhouse.com
1 3 5 7 9 10 8 6 4 2

Library of Congress Cataloging-in-Publication Data
Weston, Carrie.
If a chicken stayed for supper / by Carrie Weston ; illustrated by Sophie Fatus.
p. cm.
First published in Great Britain in 2006 by Simon and Schuster UK Ltd.
Summary: Even though they promise not to leave the den when their mother goes out hunting for a chicken for supper,
five little foxes are unable to resist going outside to play in the dark.
ISBN-13: 978-0-8234-2067-4 (hardcover)
[1. Foxes—Fiction. 2. Behavior—Fiction. 3. Chickens—Fiction. 4. Night—Fiction. 5. Lost children—Fiction.]
I. Fatus, Sophie, ill. II. Title.
PZ7.W526283Ifa 2007
[E]—dc22
2006049511

If a Chicken Stayed for Supper

by Carrie Weston

illustrated by Sophie Fatus

Holiday House / New York

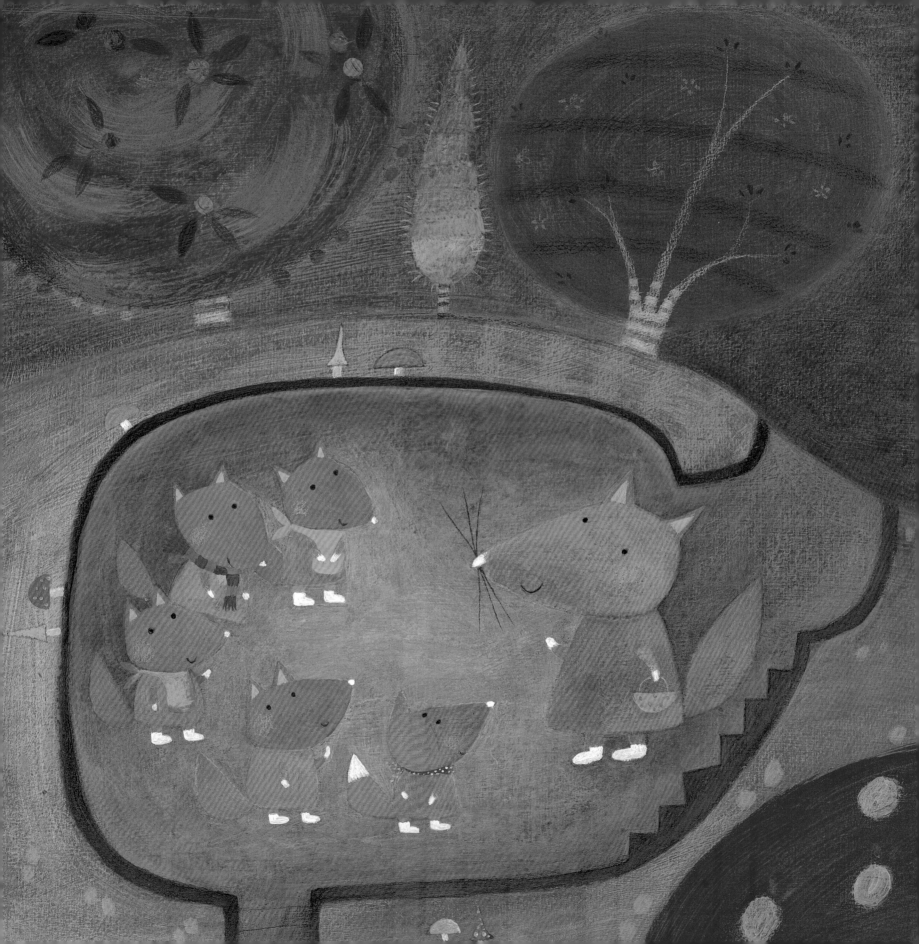

On a clear, moonlit night, Mommy Fox kissed
each of her five children good-bye.
"We will have chicken for supper tonight!" she told them.
The little foxes licked their lips and their tummies rumbled.
"Now, do not leave the den when I am gone,"
warned Mommy Fox.

"No, Mommy!" sang the five little foxes together.

The five little foxes huddled together: Tufty, Mufty, Rusty, Misty, and Rag. They waited, and they thought of chicken for supper.

They waited, and they waited.

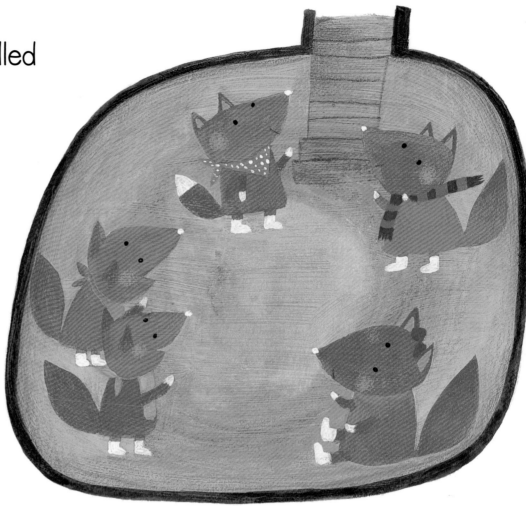

"Let's go and play!" said Rag.
"But Mommy said not to leave the den," said Tufty.
"It's very dark out there," squeaked Rusty.

"Well, *I'm* off to have fun," said Rag, and
he darted out of the den and into the night.

"I hope he'll be all right," said Rusty.
"Maybe we should follow him," said Tufty.

Each little fox crept nearer and nearer
to the hole of their den.
They sniffed the air. They looked at one another.
Then, one by one, they leapt out into the night.

They jumped.

They romped.

They rolled.

They tumbled.

They crept and they leapt.

Suddenly Tufty stopped.
"Just look at our muddy coats!" she said.

"It's so dark," squeaked Rusty.
"One of us could get lost!" said Mufty.
"One of us could *already* be lost!"
Rag laughed.

"Oh no!" said Misty. "One of us is lost in the dark!"

The little foxes began to weep.

Tufty wiped her eyes and sniffed.
"I'm the oldest," she said, "so I shall count us all."

She tapped each of their noses
in turn as she counted.
"One," she said, tapping Mufty's nose.
"Two." She tapped Misty.
"Three," she went on as she tapped Rusty.
"Four." She got to Rag.

Then she stopped.
"*Four!*" gasped Tufty.
"Oh dear! One of us *is* lost."

The little foxes
wept some more.

Then Mufty dabbed his nose.
"Let me count," he said. "I'm the second oldest."

He tugged each of their tails as he counted.
"One." He tugged Tufty's tail.
"Two." He grabbed Misty's.
"Three." He gave a pull on Rusty's tail.
"Four." He yanked Rag's.

"We used to be five and now we're only four!"
wailed Mufty.

The little foxes' weeping grew
louder and louder.
"I wish I knew how
to count," cried Rusty.

Just then Mother Hen appeared
from under a bush.
"Cluck, cluck, cluck," she said kindly,
"what is all this crying?"

"One of us is missing," sniffed Tufty.
"We used to be five and now we're four,"
stuttered Rusty.
"It's all my fault!" wailed Rag.

Then Mother Hen gently stood the little foxes in a row and patted each of their heads as she counted out loud.
"One." She patted Tufty first.
"Two." Then Mufty.
"Three." Next Rusty.
"Four." And Misty.
"Five. There." She patted Rag last.

"You've found one of us!" yelped Tufty.

"Thank you! *Thank you!*" yapped all the little foxes at once.

Mother Hen led the little foxes back to their den.

The hole at the top of the den was dark.
"We're scared," said Misty.
"Won't you come in with us?" asked Rusty.
"*Please*," begged Rag.

"Well, just for a minute or two then," said Mother Hen.
Deep, deep down into the hole she went.

At the bottom of the den
two eyes gleamed.
Sharp white teeth sparkled.
Whiskers twitched.
A wet nose sniffed the air.

"Mommy! Mommy!" yelped the little foxes together.
"Where have you been?" said a worried Mommy Fox.
She listened to their story as she stirred
a steaming pot on the fire.
"We're hungry," said Rag at last.
"I'm not surprised," said Mommy Fox,
"and all I've brought tonight are vegetables
from the farmer's field. . . ."

Mother Hen looked at Mommy Fox.
Mommy Fox looked at Mother Hen.

"... But I've made a lovely soup," said Mommy Fox, smiling,
"and there's plenty to go around."
Tufty counted out bowls for each of them.

"One. Two. Three. Four. Five. Six. . . .

So the little foxes did have a chicken
for supper that night.
And she enjoyed the soup very much indeed.

Misty

Rag

Tufty

Mufty

Rusty